MEET THE LITTLE ENGINE THAT COULD™

By Watty Piper

Illustrated by Cristina Ong

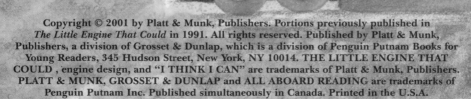

Library of Congress Catalog Card Number: 00-107520

ISBN 0-448-42482-7   F G H I J

Platt & Munk, Publishers • New York

THE LITTLE ENGINE THAT COULD™

Here comes a little red train.

Here come dolls!
Here come toys!

Chug, chug, chug.
They go in here.

Puff, puff, puff.
They come out here.

They go up the hill.

Oh, no!
Now the train is stuck!

Here comes a big train!
Will he help?

No! He will not.
He is too busy.

Here comes an old train!
Will he help?

No! He cannot.
He is too old.

Here comes a
Little Blue Engine!
Will she help?

Yes!
She is little.
But she will try.

I think I can. I think I can.
Chug, chug, chug!

I think I can. I think I can!
Puff, puff, puff!

She is at the top!

Hurray for
the Little Blue Engine!

THE LITTLE ENGINE THAT COULD™
AND THE LOST HIPPO

This is Hal.
He is a hippo.

Hal is sad.
Hal is lost.

Where is Mommy?
Where is Daddy?

Here is a train yard.
Who lives here?

The Little Blue Engine!

Hal looks and looks.

He wants to be with his
mommy and daddy.

Can the Little Blue Engine help?

Yes.
She will try.

They go over the river.

I think I can. I think I can.

They go up a hill.

Chug, chug, chug!
I think I can. I think I can!

Oh, look!
There is Mommy!
There is Daddy!

Now they go down the hill.
Puff, puff, puff.

Hal is happy!

Hurray for the Little Blue Engine!